REBECCA

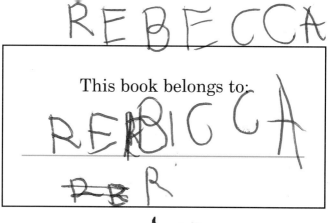

This book belongs to:

REBICCA

R B R

All Ladybird books are available at most bookshops,
supermarkets and newsagents, or can be ordered direct from:

Ladybird Postal Sales
PO Box 133 Paignton TQ3 2YP England
Telephone: (+44) 01803 554761
Fax: (+44) 01803 663394

A catalogue record for this book is available
from the British Library

Published by Ladybird Books Ltd
A subsidiary of the Penguin Group
A Pearson Company

Text © Wes Magee MCMXCVIII
Illustrations © Alex de Wolf MCMXCVIII

LADYBIRD and the device of a Ladybird are trademarks of
Ladybird Books Ltd Loughborough Leicestershire UK

Amanda
and the Pot of
Gold

by Wes Magee
illustrated by Alex de Wolf

Ladybird

"Look, Amanda!" said Grandma. "A rainbow on my birthday! There's a pot of gold at the end of the rainbow. Did you know that?"

"No, Grandma, I didn't," said Amanda.

"If I could *find* that pot of gold," thought Amanda, "it would be a perfect present for Grandma."

Amanda set off to find the end of the rainbow, where it disappeared behind a distant hill.

"Be back in time for my birthday tea," called Grandma. "And bring some friends!"

In the long lane, Amanda met Haggle the horse.

"Haggle," said Amanda, "would you like to come to Grandma's birthday tea?"

"I certainly would," neighed Haggle the horse.

"Good!" said Amanda. "But first, will you help me to find the pot of gold at the end of the rainbow? It will be a perfect present for Grandma."

"I certainly will," neighed Haggle the horse.

Down the long lane went Amanda and Haggle the horse.

At the round pond they met Crocus the cat.

"Crocus," said Amanda, "would you like to come to Grandma's birthday tea?"

"I certainly would," purred Crocus the cat.

"Good!" said Amanda. "But first, will you help us to find the pot of gold at the end of the rainbow? It will be a perfect present for Grandma."

"I certainly will," purred Crocus the cat.

Around the pond went Amanda, Haggle the horse and Crocus the cat.

At the big barn they met Shambles the sheepdog.

"Shambles," said Amanda, "would you like to come to Grandma's birthday tea?"

"I certainly would," barked Shambles.

"Good!" said Amanda. "But first, will you help us to find the pot of gold at the end of the rainbow? It will be a perfect present for Grandma."

"I certainly will," barked Shambles the sheepdog.

And what's more, I'll follow these four!

Past the big barn went Amanda the horse, Crocus the cat and, of course, Shambles the sheepdog.

It wasn't long before they came to the wood.

It was a deep, dark wood.

"The end of the rainbow is somewhere in this deep, dark wood," said Amanda.

"Looks scary in there," said Amanda.

"Very scary," purred Crocus the cat.

"Very, very scary," barked Shambles the sheepdog.

"I agree, it *is* scary," neighed Haggle the horse. "But we must go in there if we want to find the pot of gold for Grandma's birthday. Come on, follow me!"

And Haggle the horse led the way into the deep, dark wood.

Haggle the horse led Amanda, Crocus the cat and Shambles the sheepdog deeper and deeper into the dark wood.

They trooped down the twisting path.
They brushed past bushes and brambles.
They ducked beneath branches.

"Whoooo are you?" hooted an owl in a tree.
"Whoooo are you?"

They all jumped with fright.

Amanda and the animals reached a grassy glade in the middle of the wood. There they stopped and stared. They had found the end of the rainbow.

"What beautiful colours!" said Amanda.

Never mind the colours. They look fine. That pot of gold should soon be mine!

"Look! Bees!" cried Amanda.

"Hundreds!" neighed Haggle the horse.

"Thousands!" barked Shambles the sheepdog.

"And Beehives!" purred Crocus the cat.

In the grassy glade, Amanda and the animals met a man wearing a funny hat.

"Hello," said the man. "I'm the beekeeper."

"Hello," said Amanda. "We're looking for the pot of gold at the end of the rainbow, for Grandma's birthday."

The beekeeper smiled. Then he handed Amanda a big pot. It was full of honey... golden honey.

"A pot of gold!" cried Amanda. "The *honey* is the pot of gold. And Grandma loves honey. It's a perfect present for her birthday. Thank you!"

Wrong, Amanda! It's a perfect present for a fox with pink socks!

The fox with pink socks grabbed the pot of golden honey and ran into the wood.

"STOP HIM!" shouted Amanda. "Stop that fox with pink socks!"

"Don't worry," said the beekeeper. "We'll stop him."

The beekeeper lifted the lid of one of the beehives.

The buzzing bees flew after the fox with pink socks.

B

The fox with pink socks ran faster and faster.

Then suddenly he tripped…

and dropped the pot of golden honey.

BUZZZZZZZ BUZZZZZZZ

With a yelp the fox disappeared into the deep, dark wood, followed by the cloud of buzzing bees.

Carefully carrying the pot of golden honey, Amanda led Haggle the horse and Crocus the cat, followed by Shambles the sheepdog, back through the deep, dark wood.

There was no sign of the fox with pink socks.

Amanda and the animals left the deep, dark wood, went past the big barn, around the round pond, and down the long lane until they arrived at Grandma's house.

"Happy birthday, Grandma!" said Amanda.

"Happy birthday, Grandma!" said the animals.

"Oh, a pot of golden honey!" said Grandma. "What a surprise! It's a perfect present for my birthday!"